Gorp's Dream

A Tale of Diversity, Tolerance, and Love in Pumpernickel Park

Story by
Gorp
as told to
Sherri Chessen

Illustrations by
Christy Masel

The Gorp Group, LLC

We ♡ you!
GORP
Miss Sherri

Library of Congress Control Number: 2002094719

Summary: A poem promoting diversity, tolerance, love, and non-violence.

ISBN: 0-9724249-1-1

Project management by Via Press, Phoenix Arizona

Published by The Gorp Group, LLC

1-888-729-4677 (PAX-GORP)

Printed in Singapore

Note to Educators
Gorp's Dream has an accompanying teacher's guide with questions and activities based on BLOOM'S TAXONOMY OF SKILLS. Also dominant in the material are CHARACTER EDUCATION objectives, those aspects of personal development that are so vital but difficult to precisely define.

...dedicated especially to the memory of Dr. David Pent,
a truly gentle man who personified
the qualities of kindness and love.

"I had a dream just last night
about a baker and his wife.
I watched them mix their magic
when the dough all came to life!

I learned so much from each of them,
and I share it now with you.
It's just pretend,
but in the end,
may this sweet dream
come true!"

1

In a happy little neighborhood
called Pumpernickel Park
lived folks of many colors...
some white, some wheat,
some dark.

The Tortillas lived next to the Danish
with never a mean word or fight.
The Donuts had Fruit Cakes for neighbors,
they thought them a wacky delight!

WELCOME TO
PUMPERNICKEL
PARK

3

A family with dozens of cousins
were the Bagels on floor number four.
Because they respected each other
there was peace and kindness galore!

The Cookies lived next to the Pitas.
Though different in so many ways,
they shared and cared for each other.
No hatred or greed in their days!

5

The Bread Sticks were Italian,
'n' though some were very tall,
they didn't laugh at the Shortbread
for being squat and small.

A Tart lived up on the third floor,
with a Cream Puff down below.
They didn't judge each other
and always said, "Hello!"

The Fortune Cookies from China
had the Jellyrolls to their right.
Good sports is what the children were,
morning, noon and night.

7

THEN ...a crusty, cranky couple
whose favorite word was, "NO,"
moved to Pumpernickel Park.
Their name was Sourdough!

WELCOME TO
PUMPERNICKEL
PARK

The 'Doughs were mean and mouthy
to the guys and to the gals
of different races, darker faces,
and so they had no pals.

9

The first to feel their bullying
was the sweet, round English Muffin.
They laughed at her "foreign" accent
and caused her all this sufferin'.

The 'Doughs despised the Brownies
and thought them much too nutty.
"You're only right if you are white,
you'll never be our buddy!"

11

Croissant was a curvy French gal,
who liked the Jewish Ryes,
'til the 'Doughs
tried to change her mind
with a pack of ugly lies.

The only ones
the 'Doughs would like,
the only ones they'd trust,
were those they thought
just like them,
the so-called
Upper Crust!

Then one day when it was least expected,
a fire began and went undetected.
The 'Doughs left their baby with nanny Banan-y,
who only knew how to sit on her fanny.

14

She fixed her nails,
she watched TV,
she talked on the phone
and so didn't see
smoke curling up,
fire start to flicker,
Banan-y just sat there
with her hand on the clicker.

15

Smoke snaked down the hall,
and under the door
of the old, seedy Ryes,
then smoldered some more.

Mrs. Rye smelled the smoke.
It was lucky, you see,
'cause Grandma Rye coughed
and slapped her spouse on his knee!

17

She tossed back her head,
cried out with alarm,
"Let's go through the building
or the smoke could cause harm

to all of our friends
in Pumpernickel Park.
Big fires can start
from one little spark!"

Just then came a screeeeeech
like the cry of a bat.
"It's Kristi the Crispy's
calico cat!"

"Oh, no!" said motherly,
wise Mrs. Rye.
"It's the Sourdough's baby,
I know that high cry!"

19

They ran to the 'Dough's,
and called to the sitter,
who was running around
with her head all atwitter.

"Be calm...now go...call 911,
and where is the baby?
Banan-y, how come
you don't have her with you?
Now get her, just ru-u-unnn!!!!"

But Banan-y just stood there
all rigid and numb
and couldn't get moving
not one little crumb.

21

So the Ryes just took over,
though old and quite slow,
and searched for that baby
'til they saw down below...

the wee baby crib
with the wee baby girl,
who was dimpled and darling
with blue eyes and a curl.

22

But the icky, thick smoke
was starting to hover
like a cloud of gray soot
round her pink 'n' white cover!

23

So Grandmother Rye
pulled herself tall
to her full 4 feet 10
and lifted that doll

right out of her crib
and into her arms.
Baby snuggled and cooed,
safe from all harm.

24

"Cover your mouths.
Keep out of the smoke.
Stay close to the floor.
You don't want to choke."

Smart words, Poppa Rye,
Now don't be so slow.
Feel the door...it's not hot.
So keep low, and just
gooooooooo!

25

They did it just perfect
each step was just right.
But when they got to the street
they saw quite a sight.

26

The 'Doughs had arrived after parking their car,
but ran lickety-splicket when they saw from afar
that the building they lived in was billowing flame.
Their first ugly thought was, "Who is to blame?"

27

The 'Doughs couldn't believe
what they saw with their eyes.
Their baby is safe,
but is saved ...by the RYES!

They sniffled, they snuffled
gave several soft sighs,
but how to thank someone
like the old Jewish Ryes?

28

The 'Doughs watched the Ryes
as they cuddled the baby.
Their faces weren't similar,
but deep down, just maybe,

the Ryes and the 'Doughs
were exactly the same,
just different faces
and not the same name.

29

Something kerplinked
in the 'Doughs' sour soul,
for instead of a heart
was a deep, empty hole

that filled up so quickly
with love for the Ryes
they realized at last
that hating's not wise.

Bullying or teasing
or shouting bad words
at someone who's different
is just for the birds.

For faces are covers
and deep down within
lie all the same fixin's,
it's just that our skin

is often quite different
from the folks that we meet
or the children who pass us
on Poppy Seed Street!

31

"Well, that's my dream,
it's what I recall.
I hope you were listening
and remember it all.

It taught me that love
means accepting all others.
Colors don't matter,
we're sisters and brothers!

Now as you grow older
remember this tale
of the Sourdough's baby
who caused, without fail,

love and acceptance
to folks in the dark.
It's a piece of cake now
in Pumpernickel Park!"

32

P.S. ...and they lived happier...

My Promise to Gorp

Thank you, Gorp
For sharing your dream.
I know now that bullying
is ugly and mean.

Teasing's not funny
it hurts and it's cruel.
I'll be nice to all people
at home, play, or school.

I realized this fact
it's as true as can be...
When I'm nice to a person
THEY'RE NICE BACK TO ME!!!!

X _____

Please sign here if you agree with Gorp's Promise
Thank you for making this a better world!!!

Gorp was born to be a symbol for all things good and non-violent. He helps children learn lessons like respect and responsibility while being loving, kind, friendly, and fair. When Gorp isn't busy writing, helping others, or on the rainbow, he lives with Sherri Chessen, wherever she may be. Gorp loved when Sherri was a Romper Room teacher on TV, as she always saw him in the Magic Mirror!

Illustrator Christy Masel lives in Phoenix, Arizona, with her husband, Joe, and three well-fed cats. She received her Visual Communications degree from the Colorado Institute of Art in 1991 and has since illustrated six children's books and designed award-winning book covers.

Heather Potter teaches pre-school in Sun Valley, Idaho, and created the artistic concept and some of the characters for *Gorp's Dream*. Her husband Rick, daughter Breeze, and Spirit, Daisy, and Angel (dog, cat, and rabbit, respectively) make up her household.

Thank you for reading our book and for believing in Gorp.
If you'd like to know more about him, please come to his website at:
WWW.THEGORP.COM

You can also call at 1-888-729-4677 (PAX-GORP)

He even has an Email address:
gorp2@earthlink.net

We love you....
and are very proud of you for choosing to be a PEACEMAKER!

S0-CFL-839

Map Skills for Today

Grade
3

Maps Across America

Map Skills for Today
Maps Across America
Grade 3

Publisher: Keith Garton
Editorial Director: Maureen Hunter-Bone
Editorial Development: Summer Street Press, LLC
Writer: Susan Buckley
Project Editor: Miriam Aronin
Editors: Jessica Rudolph, Alex Giannini
Design and Production: Dinardo Design, LLC
Photo Editor: Kim Babbitt

Illustration Credits: Stephanie Powers
Map Credits: Mapping Specialists, Ltd.
Photo Credits: Page 4: SuperStock, John Klein/Weekly Reader; Page 6: Corbis; Page 14: Springfield, Illinois, Convention & Visitors Bureau, Alamy; Page 22: Jupiter Images; Page 23: Jupiter Images; Page 24: Photos.com; Page 41: Photos.com

Teachers: Go online to www.scholastic.com/mapskillsfortoday for teaching ideas and the answer key.

ISBN: 978-1-338-21490-1

1 2 3 4 5 6 7 8 9 10   40   23 22 21 20 19 18

Maps Across America

Table of Contents

Using Globes 4

Using Maps 6

A Key to Symbols 8

Directions In Between 10

How Far? 12

What Makes a City? 14

Counties and States 16

Exploring North America 18

Water, Water, Everywhere 20

All Kinds of Maps 22

Regions of the United States 24

The Northeast 26

The Southeast 28

The Midwest 30

The Southwest 32

The West 34

Alaska—Farthest North 36

Hawaii—Farthest South 37

Four Hemispheres 38

Lines of Latitude 40

Lines of Longitude 42

Review 44

Using Globes

Earth

Classroom Globe

Our home is planet Earth. We can use a **globe** to learn about our world. A globe is a model of Earth. Using a globe, you can see where land and water are on Earth. You can see their size, position, and shape.

The seven large land areas on Earth are **continents**. Water covers everything else. The largest bodies of water are **oceans**.

Think It Over

Why do you think some people call Earth "the big blue marble"?

Use Your Skills

Use the globes on page 5 to answer these questions.

1. Find the continent of North America on one of the globes. Draw a star on it.

2. What three oceans touch North America? Circle your answers.

   Indian Ocean   Pacific Ocean
   Atlantic Ocean   Arctic Ocean

3. The Indian Ocean touches three continents that begin with the letter A. Write their names.

   _____

   _____

North, South, East, West

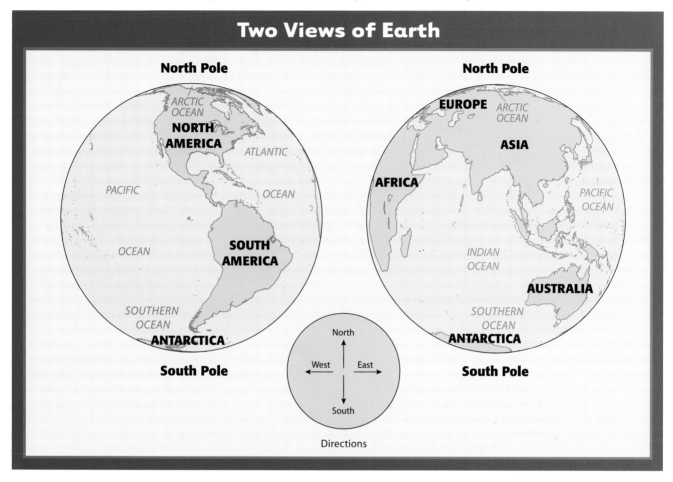

Two Views of Earth

Directions

Geographers imagine a line running through the center of Earth. They call one end the North Pole and the other end the South Pole.

Find the North Pole and the South Pole on the globes. The poles help you find **directions**. North, south, east, and west are the main directions. Geographers call these **cardinal directions**. North is the direction toward the North Pole. South is the direction toward the South Pole. When you face the North Pole, east is to your right. West is to your left.

Use Your Skills

1. Which ocean is north of North America? _____

2. Is the Indian Ocean south or east of Asia? _____

3. Is the Pacific Ocean south or west of South America? _____

4. Is the Pacific Ocean east or west of Asia? _____

Using Maps

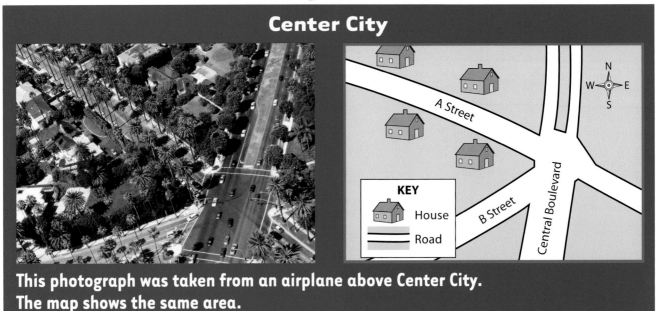

Center City

This photograph was taken from an airplane above Center City.
The map shows the same area.

Globes help us find large places on Earth. But what if you want to find something in your state or town? Then you need a map. A **map** is a picture of Earth or part of Earth from above.

You can use a map to tell directions. The **compass rose** shows you the directions on the map.

 Your Turn Now

Find a map of your community. Locate your street and your school on the map.

 **Use Your Skills**

Use the photograph and map to answer these questions.

1. Is A Street north or south of B Street? _____

2. Draw an arrow on the map to show how you would walk east on A Street and then south on Central Boulevard.

3. Find the cars in the photograph. Are they shown on the map?

_____

 **Think It Over**

Why don't maps show things that move?

Large and Small

United States

Alaska

CANADA

Washington
Montana
North Dakota
Minnesota
L. Superior
New Hampshire
Maine
Vermont
Oregon
Idaho
South Dakota
Wisconsin
L. Michigan
L. Huron
Michigan
L. Ontario
New York
Massachusetts
Rhode Island
Connecticut
Pennsylvania
New Jersey
L. Erie
Delaware
Maryland
Nevada
Wyoming
Nebraska
Iowa
Illinois
Indiana
Ohio
West Virginia
Virginia
Utah
Colorado
Kansas
Missouri
Kentucky
North Carolina
California
Mississippi R.
Tennessee
ATLANTIC OCEAN
Arizona
New Mexico
Oklahoma
Arkansas
South Carolina
Alabama
Georgia
PACIFIC OCEAN
Texas
Mississippi
Louisiana
N
W E
S
Hawaii
Florida
Gulf of Mexico

A

MEXICO

Maps can be huge or very small. They can show different-size places, too. Some show the whole world. Other maps show smaller places. Map A shows the entire United States. Map B highlights one state: Minnesota.

We use maps for many different reasons. You might use a map of the world to see where China is. You might use a street map of your town to find out how to get to the library.

Minnesota

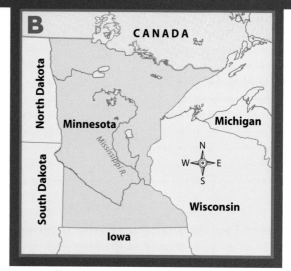

B

CANADA

North Dakota
Minnesota
Michigan
Mississippi R.
N
W E
S
South Dakota
Wisconsin
Iowa

Your Turn Now

Find a map of the world and a map of your state or town. How are they the same? How are they different?

A Key to Symbols

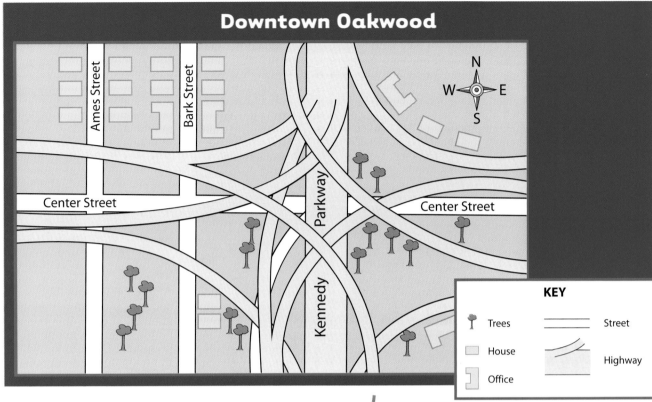

Downtown Oakwood

KEY

🌳 Trees   ──── Street

🏠 House

🏢 Office   Highway

Maps use symbols to show places and things on Earth. **Symbols** are drawings that stand for something real. A map **key** tells you what each symbol stands for.

Look at the map of downtown Oakwood. Using the key, you can find highways and streets. You can see where houses are. You can see wooded areas where trees grow. Symbols also tell you what kinds of buildings there are in downtown Oakwood.

⭐ Use Your Skills

1. 🌳 What does this symbol stand for? _____

2. What is the name of the largest roadway in downtown Oakwood? _____

3. Do more people live north or south of Center Street? _____ How can you tell? _____ _____

Map It!

Create symbols to show a school, railroad tracks, and a fire station. Add your symbols to this map.

More Map Symbols

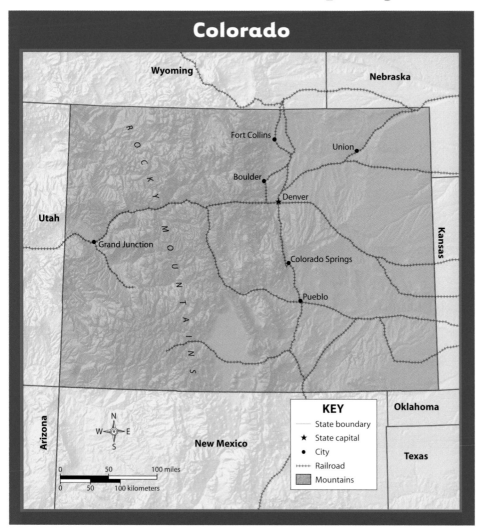

Mapmakers use symbols to show the shape of land and water. On the map, this pattern [ ] shows mountains and hills. Lines can be symbols, too. **Boundaries** are imaginary lines that divide places from one another. On this map, special lines stand for railroads.

 Use Your Skills

1. What is the capital city of Colorado? _____

2. Could you travel from Denver to Grand Junction by railroad? _____

3. What states share boundaries with Colorado? _____ _____ _____

4. Is Pueblo north or south of Fort Collins? _____

5. To get from Boulder to Union, which directions would you travel? _____

6. Where are most of the mountains in Colorado located? _____ _____

Directions In Between

Minnesota

CANADA

North Dakota

Hallock

Lake Superior

Fargo

Duluth

Michigan

Minnesota

South Dakota

Wisconsin

Minneapolis St. Paul

N

NW   NE

W   E

Rochester

SW   SE

S

Iowa

You know that the four cardinal directions are north, south, east, and west. What if a direction is between north and east? That direction is called northeast (NE). What if a direction lies between south and west? Then it is southwest (SW). Northeast and southwest are called **intermediate directions**. What are the other intermediate or "in-between" directions?

Use Your Skills

1. What direction is Duluth from Fargo? _____

2. What state is southeast of Minnesota? _____

3. What direction is Fargo from Minneapolis and St. Paul? (Hint: The answer is an intermediate direction.) _____

4. What direction is Rochester from Hallock? (Another intermediate direction) _____

Your Turn Now

Do you want a good way to remember the cardinal directions? Take this advice: *Never Eat Soggy Waffles*! Put your finger on N on the compass rose. Move clockwise around the four directions: N, E, S, W. Now make up another sentence to help you remember the directions. _____

_____

_____

Using a Highway Map

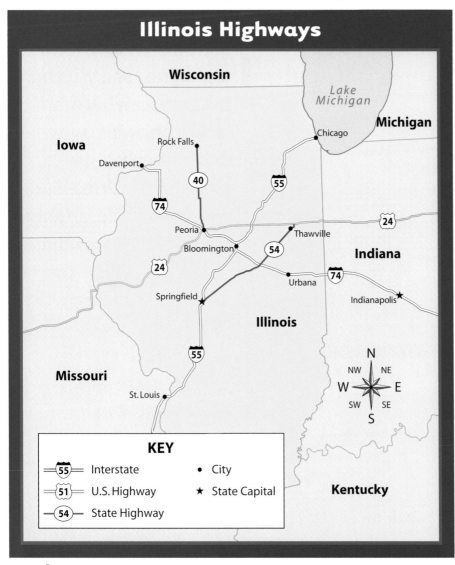

Illinois Highways

Wisconsin

Lake Michigan

Iowa

Michigan

Chicago

Rock Falls

Davenport

40

55

74

24

Peoria

Thawville

Bloomington

54

Indiana

24

74

Urbana

Springfield

Indianapolis

Illinois

55

Missouri

St. Louis

N
NW   NE
W   E
SW   SE
S

KEY

55 Interstate   • City
51 U.S. Highway   ★ State Capital
54 State Highway

Kentucky

A highway map helps you find your way when you drive. This map shows highways in the state of Illinois. Find the labels in the map key. Each label is a different shape and shows a different kind of highway. These are interstate highways, United States highways, and state highways. The highway number is always in the center of the label.

 Use Your Skills

1. Which number highways on this map are interstate highways?

   _____

   Which are state highways?

   _____

2. If you want to drive from Chicago to Peoria the shortest way, what two highways would you take?

   _____

3. If you drive from Thawville to Interstate 74, what direction do you go? (Hint: Remember to check the compass rose for cardinal and intermediate directions!) _____

   If you then turn on Interstate 74 to go to Davenport, Iowa, which direction do you go?

   _____

How Far?

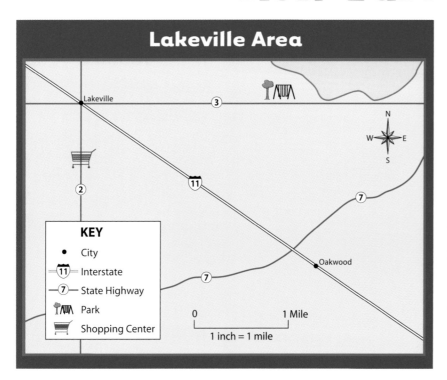

Lakeville Area

Lakeville

N
W E
S

11

7

7   Oakwood

KEY
- • City
- =11= Interstate
- -7- State Highway
- Park
- Shopping Center

0   1 Mile

1 inch = 1 mile

The best way to figure out distance on a map is by using a map scale. A **map scale** shows you what a distance on the map equals on Earth. Find the map scale on this map. It tells you that one inch on the map is the same as one mile on Earth.

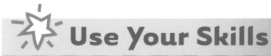
Use Your Skills

Use the map above to answer these questions.

1. What distance does one inch on the map stand for? _____

2. How many inches is the park from Lakeville on the map? _____ How many miles on Earth?

_____

3. How many miles is it from Oakwood to Lakeville? _____

4. What highway would you take from Oakwood to Lakeville?

_____

Map It!

Make up a city and show it on the map. Measure places that would be 1 mile, 2 miles, and ½ mile from the city. Show and label them on your map.

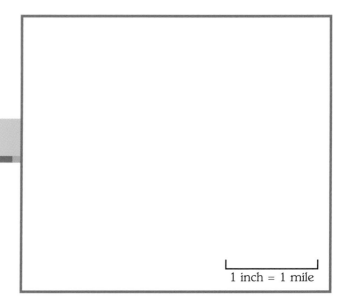

1 inch = 1 mile

Different Map Scales

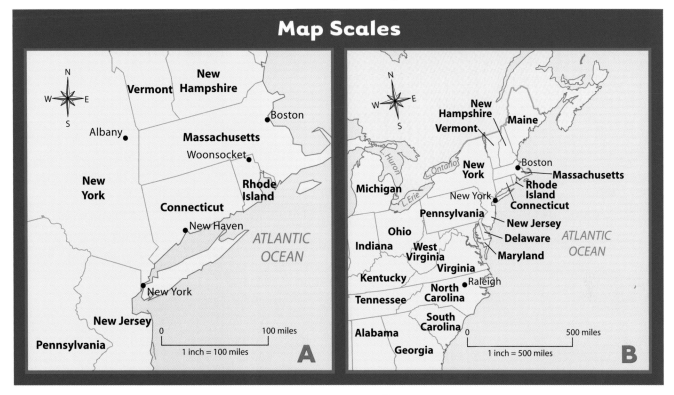

Map Scales

Map A:
New Hampshire, Vermont, Boston, Albany, Massachusetts, Woonsocket, New York, Rhode Island, Connecticut, New Haven, ATLANTIC OCEAN, New York, New Jersey, Pennsylvania

0   100 miles
1 inch = 100 miles
A

Map B:
New Hampshire, Maine, Vermont, Huron, Ontario, L. Erie, New York, Boston, Michigan, New York, Massachusetts, Rhode Island, Pennsylvania, Connecticut, Ohio, New Jersey, Indiana, West Virginia, Delaware, ATLANTIC OCEAN, Kentucky, Virginia, Maryland, Tennessee, North Carolina, Raleigh, South Carolina, Alabama, Georgia

0   500 miles
1 inch = 500 miles
B

So far you have used map scales that show that one inch on the map equals one mile. Every map has its own scale, however. Look at the two maps on this page. On Map A, the scale shows you that one inch on the map equals 100 miles on Earth. What does the scale on Map B tell you?

Use Your Skills

1. Which map would you use to measure the distance between New Haven and Woonsocket? _____

2. Which map would you use to measure the distance from Maine to Georgia? _____

3. What is the distance from Albany to New Haven? _____

Helpful Hint:
How can you measure distance on a map if you don't have a ruler? Use a piece of paper or an index card. Put the edge of the paper or card along the scale and mark off one-inch sections. Then you can use the paper or card like a ruler to measure distances on the map.

13

What Makes a City?

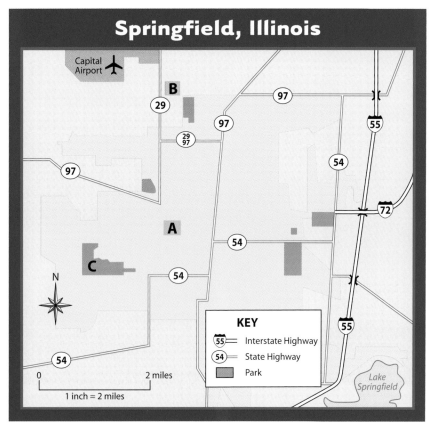

Springfield, Illinois

Capital Airport

KEY

55 Interstate Highway
54 State Highway
Park

0   2 miles

1 inch = 2 miles

Lake Springfield

N

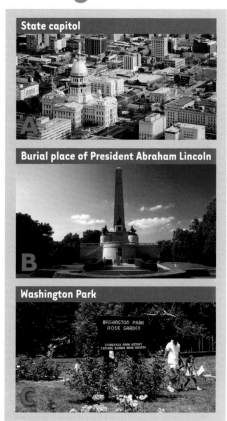

State capitol

A

Burial place of President Abraham Lincoln

B

Washington Park

C

A **city** is one kind of community. Cities have many parts: homes, stores, businesses, schools, parks, offices, theaters, government buildings, and more.

This map shows Springfield, the capital city of Illinois. A **capital** is the city where government

leaders meet. The photographs show places in Springfield. Find them on the map.

Map It!

The compass rose on the map of Springfield only shows north. Fill in the missing directions.

Use Your Skills

1. The airport is located _____ of Washington Park.

2. Lake Springfield is located _____ of the city. (Hint: This is an intermediate direction.)

3. Suppose you started at the bottom left corner of the map and took Route 54 through Springfield. You would be traveling east and _____ .

Using a City Grid

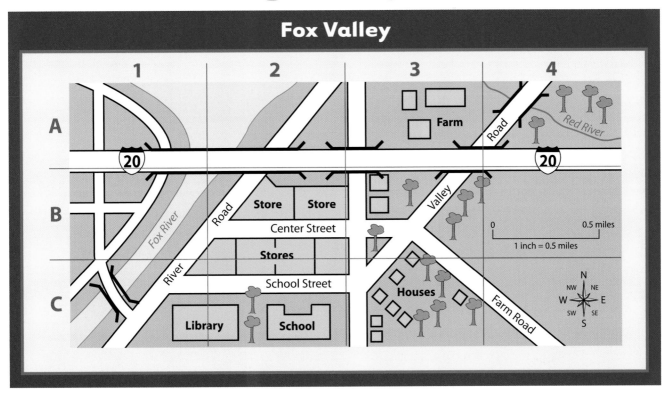

Fox Valley

A grid makes it easier to find places on a city map. A **map grid** is a series of boxes, each of which has a letter and number "address." On this map, for example, the school is in box C2.

To find a grid "address," put your finger on a letter along the side of the map. Move your finger along until you reach the correct number along the top or bottom of the map. You try it: Find box C3. What's there? (If you said "houses," you're right.)

⭐ Use Your Skills

1. Find the farm on the map. What grid box is it in? _____

2. Are there houses or stores in grid box B2? _____

3. In which two grid boxes can you locate the library? _____

4. Find the corner of School Street and Valley Road. (Hint: It's in grid box C3.) Suppose you want to drive on Valley Road to the Red River. In which direction will you drive? Use the compass rose to answer. _____

Counties and States

Delaware

Pennsylvania

Wilmington

Delaware River

New Jersey

N W E S

NEW CASTLE

0   20 miles
0   20 kilometers

Maryland

Dover ★
KENT
Delaware

Delaware Bay

ATLANTIC OCEAN

Georgetown
SUSSEX

A

KEY
★ State capital — State boundary
□ County seat — County boundary

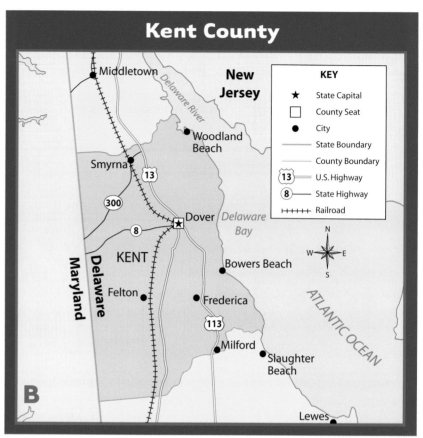

Kent County

Middletown

Delaware River

New Jersey

KEY
★ State Capital
□ County Seat
● City
— State Boundary
— County Boundary
(13) U.S. Highway
(8) State Highway
+++ Railroad

Woodland Beach

Smyrna
(13)

(300)

(8)   Dover ★   Delaware Bay

KENT

Maryland / Delaware

Felton

Bowers Beach

N W E S

Frederica

(113)

ATLANTIC OCEAN

Milford
Slaughter Beach

Lewes

B

Every state except one is divided into areas called counties. (In Louisiana, the areas are called parishes.) A **county** is the largest kind of local government in a state. Each county has a county seat. That is the city where the county government has its offices.

Your Turn Now

What county do you live in? What is the name of the county seat?

Use Your Skills

1. Pennsylvania, New Jersey, and _____ border Delaware.
   Maryland   Massachusetts

2. The eastern boundary of Kent County is _____ .
   the Delaware Bay   Maryland

3. The county seat of Sussex County is _____ .
   Georgetown   Milford   Lewes

4. If you take the train from Dover to Middletown, you pass through _____ .
   Felton   Smyrna   Frederica

Fifty States

The United States has been a country since 1776. It started out with only 13 states. Today there are 50 states in the United States.

Map It!

Find your state on the map. Draw a line around its boundaries.

Use Your Skills

Put a ✔ next to each sentence that is true about your state.

1. ___ My state is east of the Mississippi River.

2. ___ My state borders an ocean.

3. ___ My state is west of our nation's capital.

4. ___ My state is closer to Mexico than to Canada.

5. ___ My state touches one of the Great Lakes.

Circle the answer that best completes each sentence.

6. An ocean liner could dock at a harbor in _____ .
   New York   Kansas   New Mexico

7. A plane flying from Virginia to Kansas would cross the _____ .
   Gulf of Mexico   Mississippi River

8. The state of _____ is made up completely of islands.
   Alaska   Florida   Hawaii

17

Exploring North America

North America, Physical

ARCTIC OCEAN

GREENLAND
(DENMARK)

Denmark Strait

UNITED STATES
(Alaska)

Davis Strait

Hudson
Bay

CANADA

Gulf of
St. Lawrence

PACIFIC

OCEAN

Lake
Superior

Great Lakes

Lake
Huron

Lake
Ontario

Lake
Michigan

Lake
Erie

UNITED STATES

ATLANTIC

OCEAN

N
W   E
S

Gulf of California

BAHAMAS

Gulf of
Mexico

DOMINICAN
REPUBLIC

MEXICO

CUBA

HAITI

JAMAICA

KEY
— National border
▨ Mountains

BELIZE HONDURAS

Gulf of
Tehuantepec

NICARAGUA
PANAMA

GUATEMALA
EL SALVADOR

COSTA RICA

SOUTH
AMERICA

North America is the continent where the United States is located. What other countries are located on the continent of North America?

This map is a **physical map**. Physical maps show **landforms**, or the shape of the land. On page 9 you read about mountains and hills. This symbol ▨ shows mountains on the map of North America.

Plains, large areas of flat land, are another landform. They are located in the center of the United States and along the eastern and southern coasts.

Use Your Skills

1. The continent shown on the map on page 18 is _____.
   North America Asia Europe

2. Canada and _____ are north of the 48 states.
   Belize Jamaica Greenland

3. The country that borders the United States to the south is _____.

   Mexico Canada South America

4. Guatemala borders Mexico, Honduras, El Salvador, and _____.

   Cuba the United States Belize

5. _____ is the country farthest south in North America.
   Nicaragua Panama Haiti

6. Most of North America's mountains are located on the _____ side of the continent.
   eastern western northern

7. There are _____ mountains on the coast of Hudson Bay.
   few no many

8. There are _____ mountains on the southern coast of the United States.
   few no many

Using a Locator Map

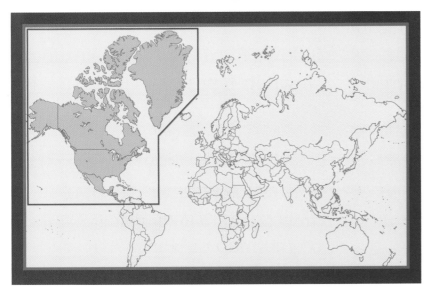

Often it helps to know where in the world a place is located. The small map on this page is called a **locator map**. The box shows the part of the world covered in the map on page 18.

Think It Over

Scientists believe that South America and Africa were once joined together. Looking at this locator map, do you think this is true? What are some clues?

Water, Water, Everywhere

Did you know that most of Earth's water is salt water in the five oceans? Fresh water can be found in lakes, rivers, and other bodies of water. A **lake** is a body of water enclosed by land. Many rivers start in lakes.

Every river flows in one main direction. The direction a river flows is called **downstream**. All rivers flow from higher to lower land. They all flow toward a larger body of water. **Brooks**, **creeks**, and **streams** are like small rivers. They may flow into larger rivers or lakes. The largest rivers flow into bays, gulfs, or oceans. A **bay** is part of an ocean or lake that is partly enclosed. Find the Roaring River on this map.

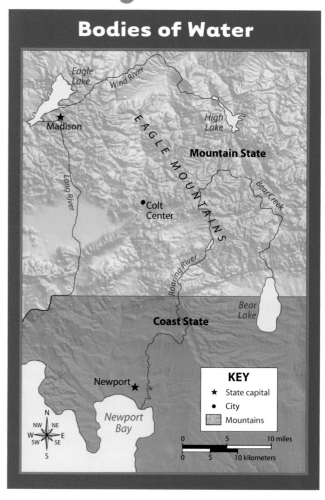

Bodies of Water

Eagle Lake
Wind River
High Lake
★ Madison
EAGLE MOUNTAINS
Mountain State
Long River
• Colt Center
Bear Creek
Roaring River
Bear Lake
Coast State
Newport ★
Newport Bay

KEY
★ State capital
• City
▨ Mountains

0   5   10 miles
0   5   10 kilometers

N NE NW E W SE SW S

It flows from the mountains into Newport Bay.

Use Your Skills

1. The Wind River begins in High Lake. What larger lake does it flow into? _____

2. Bear Creek begins in the mountains. What lake does it flow down to? _____

3. What does Roaring River flow into? _____

Think It Over

Why do you think all rivers flow from higher to lower ground?

Your Turn Now

Use a map of your state to find a lake and a river. Do any rivers flow out of the lake? Where does the river begin and end?

Texas Rivers

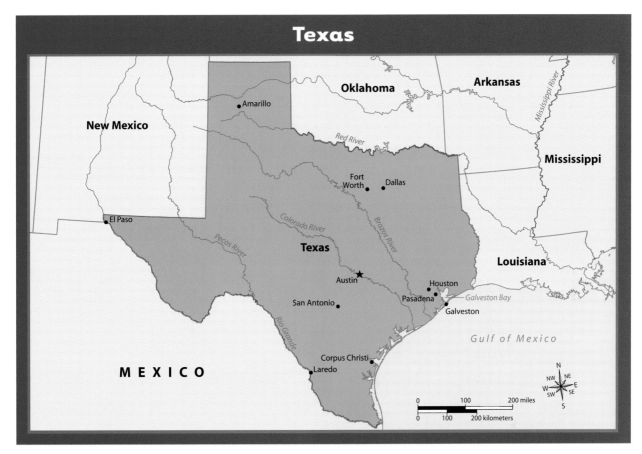

Texas

Texas is a large state with many rivers. The place where a river begins is its **source**. The place where it flows into a larger body of water is its **mouth**. This map shows rivers whose mouths are at the Gulf of Mexico. A **gulf** is a large section of an ocean.

 ## Use Your Skills

1. Find the Gulf of Mexico on the map of North America on page 18. The Gulf of Mexico is part of the _____ Ocean.

2. The city of Austin is located on the _____ River.

3. The source of the Pecos River is in _____ .

4. The _____ forms the border between Texas and Mexico.

5. The Red River flows east and _____ to the Mississippi River.

6. To get from Pasadena to the Gulf of Mexico, a ship would have to travel through _____ Bay.

All Kinds of Maps

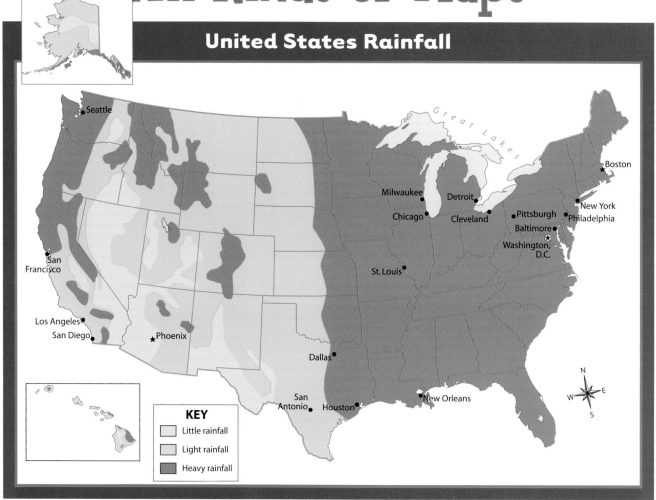

United States Rainfall

Seattle

Great Lakes

Milwaukee
Detroit
Chicago
Cleveland
Pittsburgh
New York
Philadelphia
Baltimore
Washington, D.C.
Boston

San Francisco

St. Louis

Los Angeles
San Diego
Phoenix

Dallas

San Antonio
Houston
New Orleans

N
W E
S

KEY
Little rainfall
Light rainfall
Heavy rainfall

Every map has a purpose—to give you information. There are many kinds of maps. Maps that help you locate cities, states, and countries are called **political maps**. **Landform maps** tell you about the shape of the land.

This map is a **climate map**. Climate is the weather over a period of time. Different places in the United States have very different climates. Some receive large amounts of rain and snow.

Others are hot and dry all year long. This map shows rainfall in the United States. The map key tells you what each color stands for.

Seattle, Washington, is famous for its rainy climate.

Use the map on page 22 to answer these questions.

1. What does the brownish color stand for on the map? _____

2. Does San Diego, California, get little, light, or heavy rainfall?

   _____

3. Is there more rainfall in the eastern half or the western half of the country? _____

4. Which city has the most rainfall: Boston, San Antonio, or Los Angeles? _____

5. Which city on the map receives the least rainfall? _____

6. Do the cities around the Great Lakes get heavy or light rainfall?

   _____

7. How many states include areas that get all three amounts of rainfall? _____

 Think It Over

1. Look at the map on page 22. Are there more cities in areas with little rainfall or heavy rainfall? Why might people prefer to live in these areas?

2. The map on page 22 gives you information about rainfall in the United States. What other kinds of information might you learn from special maps?

The area around Phoenix, Arizona, receives very little rainfall.

Regions of the United States

United States Regions

Alaska

CANADA

Washington
Montana
North Dakota
Minnesota
L. Superior
New Hampshire
Vermont
Maine

Oregon
Idaho
South Dakota
Wisconsin
L. Michigan
Michigan
L. Huron
L. Ontario
L. Erie
New York
Massachusetts
Rhode Island
Connecticut

Wyoming
Iowa
Pennsylvania
New Jersey

Nevada
Nebraska
Illinois
Indiana
Ohio
Washington, D.C.
West Virginia
Delaware
Maryland

San Francisco
Utah
Colorado
Kansas
Missouri
Kentucky
Virginia

California
Mississippi R.
Tennessee
North Carolina

Arizona
New Mexico
Oklahoma
Arkansas
South Carolina
ATLANTIC OCEAN

PACIFIC OCEAN
Alabama
Georgia
Mississippi

Texas
Louisiana

KEY
- Northeast
- Southeast
- Midwest
- Southwest
- West

Hawaii
PACIFIC OCEAN

Florida

Gulf of Mexico

MEXICO

0   250   500 miles
0   250   500 kilometers

The United States is a huge country. Its 50 states touch three different oceans. To drive from Washington, D.C., near the Atlantic Ocean, to San Francisco, California, near the Pacific Ocean, is a distance of more than 2,800 miles.

To understand this big country, it helps to look at its regions. A **region** is an area that shares features. Mapmakers divide the United States into five regions. The states in each region share certain features. You will learn more about each region in this book.

The Midwest region includes many farms.

States of the Northeast	States of the Southeast	States of the Midwest	States of the Southwest	States of the West
Maine	West Virginia	North Dakota	Arizona	Washington
Vermont	Virginia	South Dakota	New Mexico	Oregon
New Hampshire	Kentucky	Minnesota	Oklahoma	California
Massachusetts	Tennessee	Wisconsin	Texas	Idaho
Connecticut	North Carolina	Michigan		Montana
Rhode Island	South Carolina	Nebraska		Wyoming
New York	Georgia	Iowa		Nevada
Pennsylvania	Florida	Illinois		Utah
New Jersey	Alabama	Indiana		Colorado
Delaware	Mississippi	Ohio		Alaska
Maryland	Louisiana	Kansas		Hawaii
	Arkansas	Missouri		

Use Your Skills

Use the map on page 24 and the chart above to fill in the blanks.

1. Wyoming is in the _____ region.

2. Alaska is in the _____ region.

3. The _____ and _____ regions have the most states.

4. The _____ region has the fewest states.

5. The Great Lakes touch the Northeast region and the _____ region.

Map It!

1. Find your state on the map on page 24. Draw a line around its boundaries. What region is your state in?_____

2. On the map, put a ★ on each state that shares a boundary with your state. How many of them are in the same region?

_____

Think It Over

Think about all of the states in your region. What features do you think they share?

The Northeast

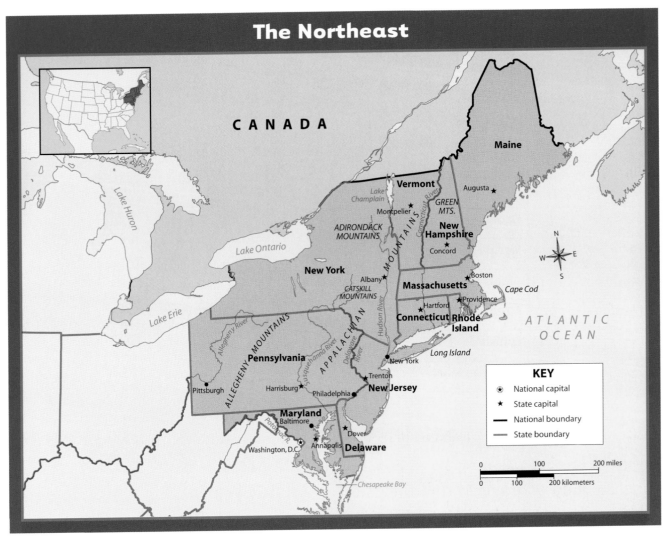

The Northeast

CANADA

Lake Huron

Lake Ontario

Lake Erie

Maine

Augusta ★

Vermont

Lake Champlain

GREEN MTS.

Montpelier ★

Connecticut River

New Hampshire

ADIRONDACK MOUNTAINS

★ Concord

New York

MOUNTAINS

Albany ★

★ Boston

CATSKILL MOUNTAINS

Massachusetts

Cape Cod

Hudson River

★ Hartford

Providence

ATLANTIC OCEAN

Allegheny River

APPALACHIAN MOUNTAINS

Susquehanna River

Delaware River

Connecticut

Rhode Island

ALLEGHENY MOUNTAINS

Pennsylvania

Long Island

New York

Pittsburgh

Harrisburg ★

Philadelphia

Trenton ★

New Jersey

Maryland

Baltimore

★ Dover

Potomac R.

Washington, D.C. ⊛

Annapolis ★

Delaware

Chesapeake Bay

KEY
⊛ National capital
★ State capital
— National boundary
— State boundary

0   100   200 miles
0   100   200 kilometers

The Northeast is the smallest region in land area. Many of the country's largest cities are there, however. New York, Philadelphia, Baltimore, and Boston are the region's largest cities.

Think It Over

Are there more cities near the coast or in the mountain areas of the Northeast? Why?

Use Your Skills

1. The Northeast region borders the _____ Ocean.

2. _____ is the capital of Massachusetts.

3. Baltimore is _____ of New York.

4. _____ is the state farthest north in the region. _____ is the state farthest south.

Exploring New York State

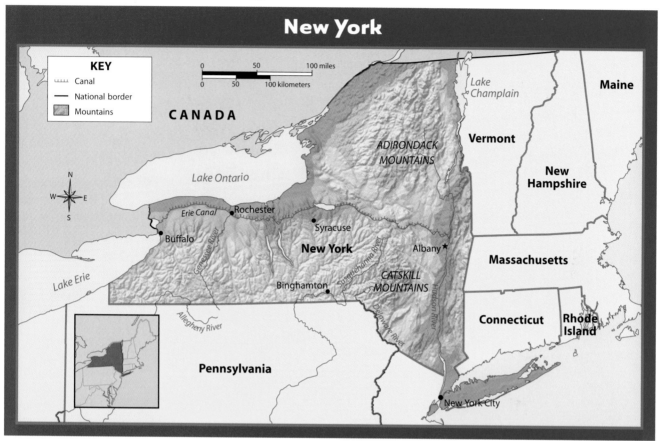

New York

KEY
- ⊔⊔⊔ Canal
- — National border
- Mountains

0   50   100 miles
0   50   100 kilometers

CANADA

Lake Champlain

Maine

ADIRONDACK MOUNTAINS

Vermont

New Hampshire

Lake Ontario

N
W E
S

Erie Canal   Rochester

Buffalo

Genesee River

Syracuse

New York

Susquehanna River

Albany ★

Massachusetts

Lake Erie

Binghamton

CATSKILL MOUNTAINS

Delaware River

Hudson River

Connecticut

Rhode Island

Allegheny River

Pennsylvania

New York City

New York is BIG! It has the largest land area of any state in the Northeast. And New York City has the largest population of any city in the United States.

Two groups of mountains run through New York. They are called the Adirondack Mountains and the Catskill Mountains.

Did you know that ships used to travel from New York City to Lake Erie? In the 1800s the Erie Canal was built. A **canal** is a waterway made by people.

Use Your Skills

1. Which two Great Lakes border New York State? _____

_____

2. What other country borders New York State? _____

3. What river connects New York City to the Erie Canal? _____

4. Are the Adirondack and Catskill mountains in the eastern or the western part of the state?

_____

27

The Southeast

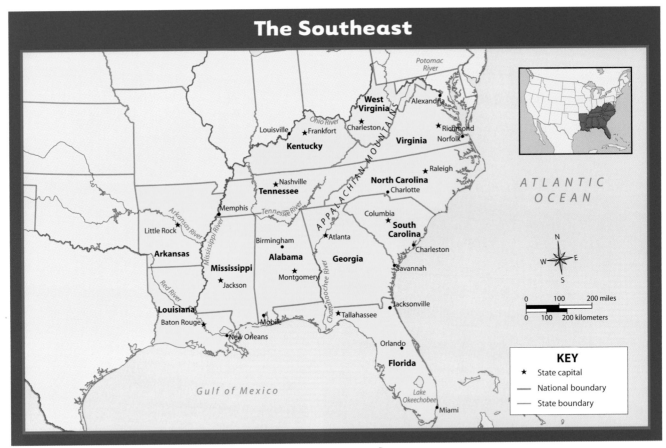

The Southeast

Potomac River
West Virginia ★
★ Alexandria
Louisville ● ★Frankfort Charleston ★ ★Richmond
Kentucky Virginia Norfolk
Ohio River
APPALACHIAN MOUNTAINS
★ Raleigh
●Nashville North Carolina
Tennessee ● Charlotte
Memphis ● Tennessee River Columbia ★
Little Rock ★ South Carolina
Arkansas River Birmingham ● ★Atlanta ● Charleston
Arkansas Alabama Georgia
Mississippi Chattahoochee River ● Savannah
★ Jackson Montgomery ★
Red River ●Jacksonville
Louisiana Mobile ● ★Tallahassee
Baton Rouge★ ●New Orleans Orlando ●
Gulf of Mexico Florida
Lake Okeechobee ● Miami

ATLANTIC OCEAN

N
W ◆ E
S

0   100   200 miles
0   100   200 kilometers

KEY
★ State capital
— National boundary
— State boundary

Water shapes the Southeast region. It is bordered by the Atlantic Ocean, the Gulf of Mexico, the great Mississippi River, and the Ohio River. Jacksonville, Memphis, Charlotte, and Louisville are the region's largest cities.

Think It Over

The Southeast has a long growing season—the time when it is warm enough for crops to grow. Why do you think the growing season there is longer than in the Northeast?

Use Your Skills

1. The land is flat along the Atlantic Ocean and the Gulf of _____ .

2. Columbia is the capital of _____ .

3. The Mississippi River forms part of the boundaries of Kentucky, Tennessee, Arkansas, _____ , and _____ .

4. The main group of mountains in the Southeast is called the _____ Mountains.

Exploring Mississippi

The "mighty Mississippi"—that's the second longest river in the United States. The state of Mississippi takes its name from the river. It is bordered by the river on its western side.

Other rivers are important in the state of Mississippi, too. The map shows six rivers that have their source in the state. Where are their mouths?

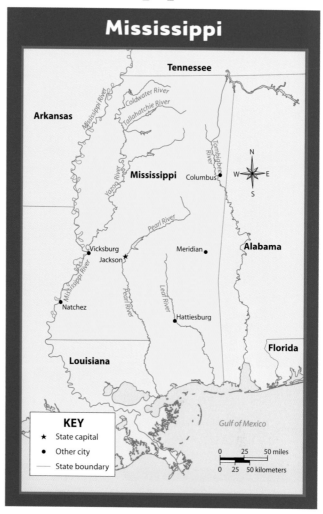

Mississippi

Use Your Skills

1. The _____ of the Tombigbee River is in Mississippi but its _____ is in Alabama.

2. The _____ River and the _____ River form part of the boundary between Louisiana and Mississippi.

3. Mississippi's capital is located on the _____ River.

4. The mouth of the Mississippi River is in the state of _____ .

Think It Over

The name *Mississippi* comes from a Native American word meaning "father of waters." Why do you think Native Americans called the river by that name?

 Your Turn Now

On the map of the United States on page 24, trace the path of the Mississippi from its source to its mouth. Research Mississippi River facts and make a chart about the river.

The Midwest

The Midwest

The Midwest has two "greats"—the Great Lakes and the Great Plains. It has big cities, big farms, and big factories, too. Chicago, Detroit, Indianapolis, and Columbus are the region's four largest cities.

 Your Turn Now

Pick a city in the Midwest that you would like to visit. Research the city. Then make a postcard to tell about your "trip."

 **Use Your Skills**

1. Four of the five Great Lakes border the Midwest. Which does not?
Lake Superior   Lake Ontario

2. The source of the Mississippi River is in this state.
Wisconsin   Minnesota

3. This river forms part of the southern boundary of the Midwest.
Ohio River   Mississippi River

4. This city is the capital of Iowa.
Springfield   Des Moines

Exploring Iowa

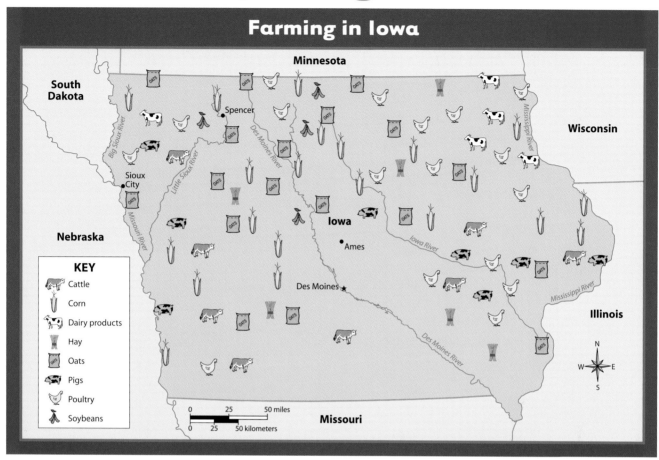

Farming in Iowa

Iowa is "farm country." Much of the land in the state is used for growing crops.

Corn is Iowa farmers' main crop. In one recent year, they grew more than 2 billion bushels of corn! Use the map key to learn where corn and other farm products are grown or raised.

Think It Over

Most of the nation's wheat is grown in the Midwest. Why do you think the region is sometimes called "the breadbasket of America"?

Use Your Skills

1. What animals are raised in Iowa?

2. What crops are grown near Spencer, Iowa? _____

3. Are more pig-raising areas found in the northern or southern part of Iowa?_____

4. Are there more poultry farms east of the Des Moines River or west of the Des Moines River?

31

The Southwest

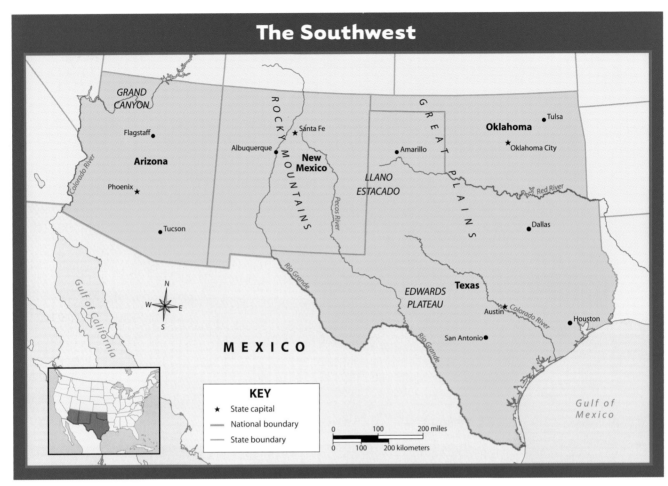

The Southwest

GRAND CANYON

Flagstaff •

Arizona

Phoenix ★

• Tucson

Colorado River

Gulf of California

MEXICO

★ Santa Fe

Albuquerque •

New Mexico

R O C K Y   M O U N T A I N S

Pecos River

LLANO ESTACADO

Rio Grande

EDWARDS PLATEAU

Rio Grande

G R E A T   P L A I N S

• Amarillo

Oklahoma

• Tulsa

★ Oklahoma City

Red River

• Dallas

Texas

Austin ★ Colorado River

San Antonio •

• Houston

Gulf of Mexico

N
W   E
S

KEY
★ State capital
— National boundary
— State boundary

0   100   200 miles
0   100   200 kilometers

The Southwest is the nation's driest region. In much of the region, the average rainfall is less than 20 inches a year. Rich in oil and other resources, the region has four of the nation's ten largest cities: Houston, Phoenix, San Antonio, and Dallas.

City	Population in 2009*
Houston, Texas	2,257,926
Phoenix, Arizona	1,601,587
San Antonio, Texas	1,373,668
Dallas, Texas	1,299,543

* Source: U.S. Census

☆ Use Your Skills

Use the map and the table to answer these questions.

1. What city is the capital of Texas?

_____

2. Which city is larger, Houston or Phoenix? _____

3. In which state is the Grand Canyon located? _____

4. What river forms the border between Texas and Mexico?

_____

Exploring Arizona

In every state, some parts have more rainfall than others during the year. Overall, Arizona is a very dry state. It even includes deserts. A **desert** is a place where very little rain or snow falls. But even in Arizona, there are a few areas where there is plenty of rain.

This map tells you about rainfall within Arizona. Look at the key. Which color shows the most rainfall?

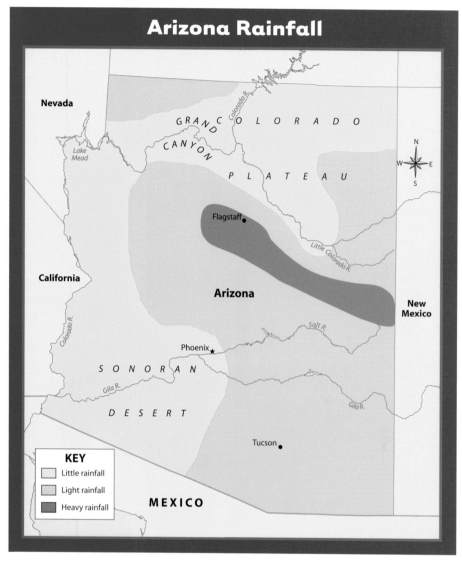

Arizona Rainfall

Nevada

Lake Mead

California

GRAND CANYON

COLORADO

PLATEAU

Colorado R.

Flagstaff

Little Colorado R.

Arizona

New Mexico

Colorado R.

Salt R.

Phoenix

SONORAN

Gila R.

DESERT

Gila R.

Tucson

KEY
- Little rainfall
- Light rainfall
- Heavy rainfall

MEXICO

 Use Your Skills

Circle T if the statement is true.
Circle F if it is false.

1. Most of Arizona has heavy rainfall. T F

2. The eastern half of Arizona is the driest part. T F

3. The capital of Arizona is in an area with little rainfall. T F

4. Flagstaff gets less rainfall than Tucson. T F

5. Tucson is probably located in a desert. T F

 Think It Over

The Southwest is part of an area sometimes called "the Sunbelt." Why do you think the area has this name?

The West

The West stretches from the Pacific Ocean to the Rocky Mountains and from Canada to Mexico. It includes areas that get a lot of rainfall and areas that are very dry. The region's largest cities are in California.

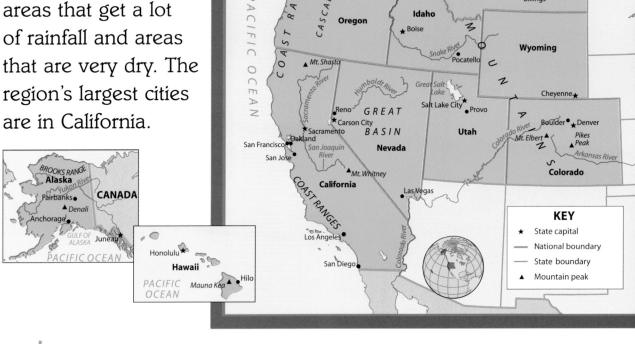

Use Your Skills

1. What mountains run through the western part of this region? _____

2. What five states border the Pacific Ocean? _____

3. What city is the capital of Oregon? _____

4. Is Boise north or south of Salt Lake City? _____
   Is it east or west of Portland? _____

Think It Over

Are there more cities in California or in Nevada? Why do you think that is true?

Exploring Washington

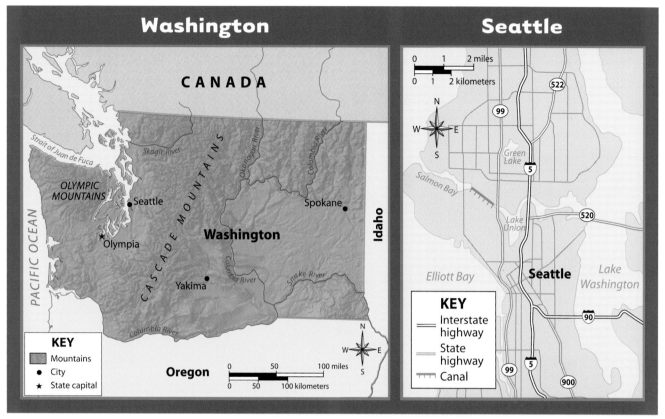

Washington

CANADA

Strait of Juan de Fuca

OLYMPIC MOUNTAINS

PACIFIC OCEAN

Skagit River

Okanogan River

Columbia River

Seattle

Spokane

Olympia

Washington

CASCADE MOUNTAINS

Yakima

Columbia River

Snake River

Idaho

Columbia River

Oregon

KEY
- Mountains
- City
- ★ State capital

0 50 100 miles
0 50 100 kilometers

Seattle

0 1 2 miles
0 1 2 kilometers

522

99

Green Lake

5

Salmon Bay

Lake Union

520

Elliott Bay

Seattle

Lake Washington

90

99 5

900

KEY
- Interstate highway
- State highway
- Canal

The Columbia River flows through the state of Washington to the Pacific Ocean. Bays on the ocean make excellent harbors. Seattle is Washington's largest and most important city. Lakes, bays, and canals link the city to the ocean.

 **Map It!**

Find and number one example of each place on one of the maps.

1. An ocean
2. A river
3. A lake
4. A bay
5. A mountain range

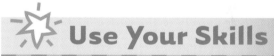 **Use Your Skills**

Use both maps on this page to fill in the blanks.

1. The _____ Mountains divide the eastern and western halves of Washington.

2. The Columbia River forms part of the boundary between Washington and _____ .

3. Green Lake in Seattle is just east of Route _____ .

4. In Seattle, Salmon Bay and Lake Union are connected by a _____ .

Alaska-Farthest North

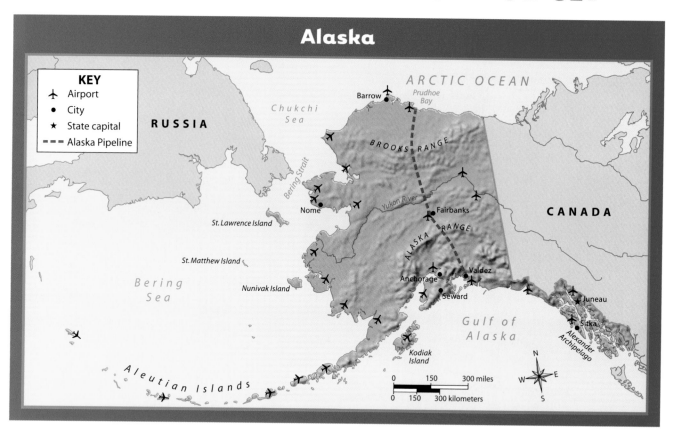

Alaska is the largest state in land area in the United States. It also is the farthest north and the coldest! It was the 49th state to become part of our country.

An enormous pipeline carries oil from oil wells in Alaska to the coast. There, ships take the oil to "the lower 48" and other countries.

Use Your Skills

1. Kodiak Island is in the _____ of Alaska.

2. The Alaska Pipeline runs from Prudhoe Bay to _____ .

3. There are two _____ near Nome, Alaska.

Fill in the correct direction—north, south, east, or west.

4. The Brooks Range of mountains is _____ of the Alaska Range.

5. The Yukon River flows _____ to its mouth.

6. Airplanes flying from Juneau to Fairbanks fly _____ .

7. Russia is _____ of Alaska.

Think It Over

Why do you think many Alaskans travel in airplanes?

Hawaii-Farthest South

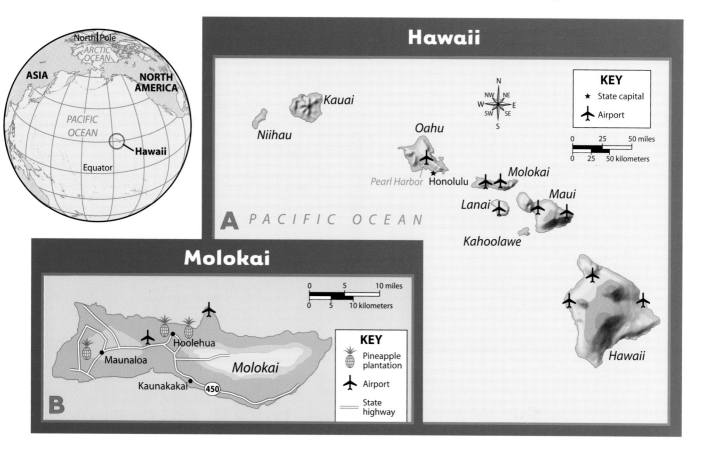

Hawaii is our "island state." This map shows the main islands, but there are many more. The state is made up of more than 100 islands. Hawaii was the 50th state to join the United States. It is further south than any other state.

⭐ Use Your Skills

Which map on this page, A or B, could help you find this information? Write the map, then the answer.

1. The largest Hawaiian island _____
   _____

2. The capital of Hawaii _____

3. An important crop on Molokai
   _____

4. The distance between Maui and Oahu _____

5. Pearl Harbor's location _____
   _____

6. The island with the most airports
   _____

Four Hemispheres

The Northern Hemisphere and the Southern Hemisphere

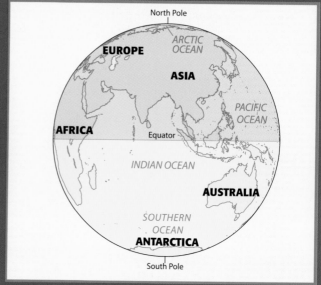

You already know about the North Pole and the South Pole. They are located at the farthest north and south points on Earth. Exactly in between the North Pole and the South Pole, an imaginary circle runs around the planet. This circle is called the **equator**.

Mapmakers use the equator to divide the Earth into two equal parts. One half is north of the equator. It includes the North Pole. This half is called the **Northern Hemisphere**. The other half is south of the equator. It is called the **Southern Hemisphere**. Here, the Northern Hemisphere and the Southern Hemisphere are shown in different colors.

Use Your Skills

1. The South Pole is in the _____ Hemisphere.
   Southern   Southwestern

2. The _____ divides the Northern Hemisphere and the Southern Hemisphere.
   North Pole   equator

3. The equator passes through the continents of South America, Asia, and _____ .
   Africa   Australia

4. The continent of _____ is located completely in the Northern Hemisphere.
   Asia   Europe

The Eastern Hemisphere and the Western Hemisphere

The Eastern and Western Hemispheres

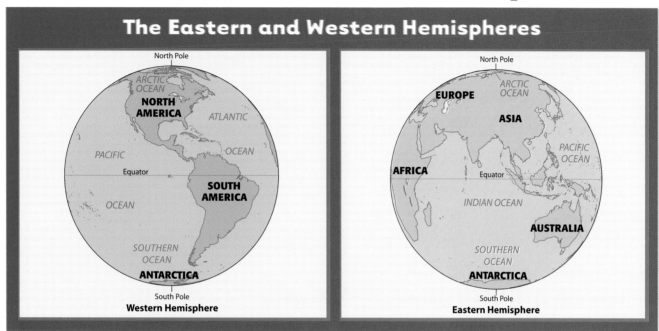

Mapmakers divide the globe at the equator to create the Northern and Southern hemispheres. They can also divide it in a different way to create the **Eastern Hemisphere** and the **Western Hemisphere**.

Think It Over

1. *Hemisphere* means half a sphere. (A sphere is a ball.) Why might people use this word to refer to how Earth is divided?

2. The United States is located in two different hemispheres. How can this be true? (Hint: Look at the maps on both pages.)

Use Your Skills

1. Is the Indian Ocean located in the Eastern Hemisphere or the Western Hemisphere? _____

2. Which continents are located completely in the Western Hemisphere? _____ _____

3. Which ocean is located entirely in the Western Hemisphere? _____

4. Use the Eastern Hemisphere and the Western Hemisphere to describe where the Pacific Ocean is located. _____ _____

Lines of Latitude

The equator is not the only imaginary line mapmakers use. They also use lines north and south of the equator to help locate places on Earth. These are called lines of **latitude**. Lines of latitude circle the globe and are parallel to each other. That means that the lines are always the same distance apart. They never meet. Sometimes lines of latitude are also called **parallels**.

The equator is a very special parallel. It is the starting point for measuring latitude. The equator is also called 0°. Distance north or south from the equator is measured in degrees (°). For example, the North Pole is at 90°N. That means it is 90° north of the equator. A place halfway between the equator and the North Pole would be at latitude 45°N. Latitudes south of the equator are marked like this: 60°S.

Lines of latitude are not all the same size. The ones near the poles are smaller than the ones near the equator. Why do you think this is true?

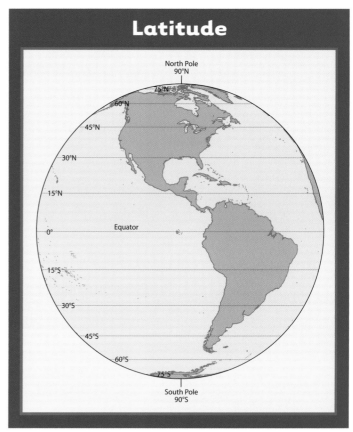

Latitude

Map It!

1. Draw a star on the line of latitude 60°N.

2. Draw a line on the map from the equator to the South Pole. What lines of latitude does it cross?

3. Trace over the lines of latitude north of the equator in red. Trace over the parallels south of the equator in blue.

Use Your Skills

1. Which direction would you go to get from the equator to 30°S?

   _____

2. Which direction would you go to get from 15°N to the equator?

   _____

3. Which line of latitude is farther away from the equator: 30°N or 45°S? _____

4. Which line of latitude is farther away from the equator: 60°N or 60°S? _____

   _____

5. In which hemisphere would you find the parallel 15°S?

   _____

6. What is the longest line of latitude? _____

 ## Think It Over

1. Could there be a line of latitude numbered larger than 90°N or 90°S? Why or why not?

2. If you were traveling straight along one line of latitude, in what direction might you be going? (Hint: There are two possible answers.)

Most penguins, like these Gentoos, live between 45°S and 60°S.

Lines of Longitude

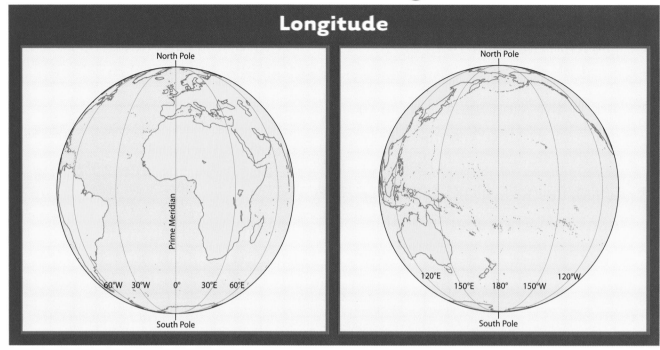

Longitude

North Pole · Prime Meridian · South Pole · 60°W · 30°W · 0° · 30°E · 60°E

North Pole · South Pole · 120°E · 150°E · 180° · 150°W · 120°W

Suppose you want to find a certain place on a map. You know that its latitude is 30°N. However, many locations have that exact same latitude. A place at 30°N might be in Florida—or in northern Africa! Latitude tells you only how far north or south of the equator a place is located. However, **longitude** can help you find its location east or west.

Longitude is different from latitude in important ways. Unlike lines of latitude, lines of longitude come together. As they approach the North Pole and the South Pole, the lines get closer together. They finally meet at the two poles.

Latitude and longitude are similar in some ways. Like latitude, longitude is measured starting from a line called 0°. Lines of longitude move away from 0° in opposite directions. However, the two directions of longitude meet again. Both directions end at 180°—the line located on the exact opposite side of the world from longitude line 0°.

All longitude lines are located between 0° and 180°. Lines of longitude going west are marked like this: 90°W. The line 90°W is located 90° west of 0°—exactly halfway between 0° and 180°. Longitude lines going east are marked like this: 90°E.

A Grid Across the Globe

You already know about map grids. You can look at page 15 to review what you have learned. Latitude and longitude also form a grid across the globe. To write the location of a place, give its latitude first and then its longitude. For example, the city of New Orleans, Louisiana, is located at latitude 30°N and longitude 90°W. So New Orleans is at 30°N, 90°W.

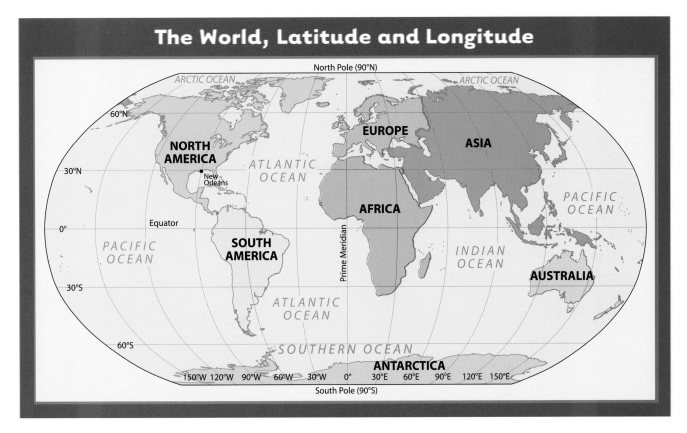

The World, Latitude and Longitude

⭐ Use Your Skills

Find each point using its latitude and longitude. Mark it on the map. Then write the continent or ocean where it is located.

1. 30°N, 30°W _____

2. 0°, 30°E _____

3. 90°S, 120°W _____

4. 30°S, 60°W _____

5. 30°N, 150°W _____

6. 30°S, 150°E _____

7. 60°N, 120°E _____

8. 90°N, 0° _____

Review

The United States

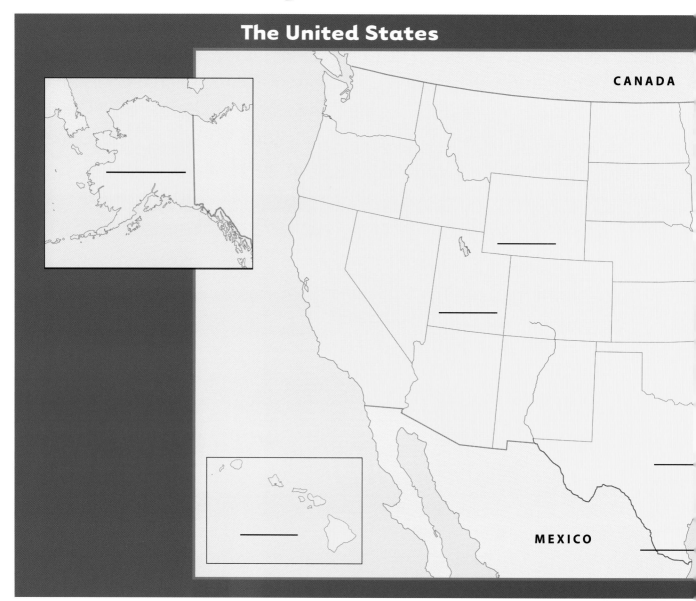

 Map It!

Write the numbers of the following locations on the blanks on Map A.

1. The nation's capital (Washington, D.C.)

2. The river that flows from Minnesota to the Gulf of Mexico (Mississippi River)

3. The most northern state (Alaska)

4. The river that borders Texas (the Rio Grande)

5. The state that contains the Great Salt Lake (Utah)

A

6. The largest of the 48 connected
   states (Texas)

7. The largest mountain range
   (Rocky Mountains)

8. The state that is located in
   the Pacific Ocean (Hawaii)

9. The five Great Lakes
   (Superior, Ontario, Erie,
   Michigan, Huron)

10. The region shown in detail
    on Map B on page 46
    (New England)

Review

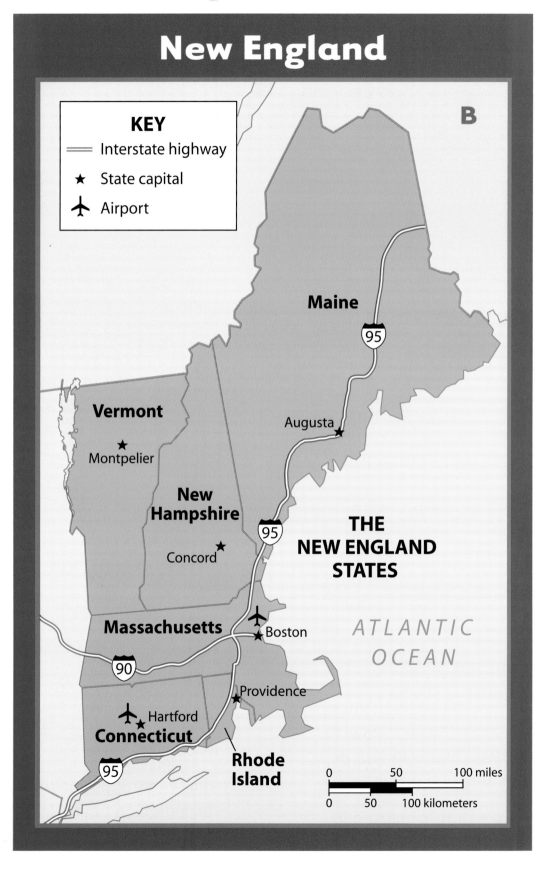

New England

KEY
- Interstate highway
- ★ State capital
- ✈ Airport

B

Maine

🛣 95

Vermont
★
Montpelier

Augusta ★

New Hampshire

Concord ★

🛣 95

THE NEW ENGLAND STATES

Massachusetts

✈ Boston ★

🛣 90

ATLANTIC OCEAN

Providence ★

✈ Hartford
★
Connecticut

🛣 95

Rhode Island

0   50   100 miles
0   50   100 kilometers

Comparing Maps

Use Your Skills

Use Map B on page 46 to answer questions 1–4.

1. What is the capital city of Vermont?

_____

2. What two New England cities show airports?

_____

_____

3. If you wanted to travel north from Boston, which interstate highway would you take?

_____

4. If you continued traveling north on this highway, what city would you reach?

_____

Look at Map A on pages 44–45 and Map B on page 46. Which map—A or B—shows each of the following?

5. The location of Providence

_____

6. An airport in Connecticut

_____

7. The three states that make up the West Coast

_____

8. The interstate highway that runs north and south along the New England coast

_____

9. The names of the New England states

_____

10. The state of Alaska

_____

11. That Maine is the most northeastern state

_____

12. What countries border the United States?

_____

Notes